TEA with MILK

ALLEN SAY

HOUGHTON MIFFLIN COMPANY BOSTON 1999

Walter Lorraine Books

Walter Lorraine (wл) Books

Copyright © 1999 by Allen Say

Library of Congress Cataloging-in-Publication Data

Say, Allen.
   Tea with milk / by Allen Say.
      p.   cm.
   Summary: After growing up near San Francisco, a young Japanese
woman returns with her parents to their native Japan, but she feels
foreign and out of place.
   ISBN 0-395-90495-1
   1. Japan—Juvenile fiction.   [1. Japan—Fiction.
2. Homesickness—Fiction.]   I. Title.
PZ7.S2744Te   1999   98-11667
[E]—dc21   CIP
                                              AC

Printed in the United States of America
HOR 10 9 8 7 6 5 4 3 2 1

For Saito Misako Sensei

From the window in her room, the girl could see the city of San Francisco. She imagined that it was a city of many palaces. And one day her father would take her there, he had promised, riding on a paddle steamer across the shining bay.

Her parents called her Ma-chan, which was short for Masako, and spoke to her in Japanese. Everyone else called her May and talked with her in English.

At home she had rice and miso soup and plain green tea for breakfast. At her friends' houses she ate pancakes and muffins and drank tea with milk and sugar.

When she graduated from high school, she wanted to go to college and then live in San Francisco. But her parents were homesick and decided to return to Japan, which was their homeland. The daughter was sad. She did not want to leave the only home she had ever known.

Once they arrived in Japan, she felt even worse. Her new home was drafty, with windows made of paper. She had to wear kimonos and sit on floors until her legs went numb. No one called her May, and Masako sounded like someone else's name. There were no more pancakes or omelets, fried chicken or spaghetti. I'll never get used to this place, she thought with a heavy heart.

Worst of all, Masako had to attend high school all over again. To learn her own language, her mother said. She could not make friends with any of the other students; they called her *gaijin* and laughed at her. *Gaijin* means "foreigner."

The woman who taught English conversation did not seem much older than Masako. Maybe she'll be my friend, Masako thought. But the teacher refused to speak English with her. She could not teach an American, she said.

So Masako wandered around the empty schoolyard. Small singsong voices came drifting from the classroom, chanting kindergarten English. She wanted to shout at them, "I know the words you are learning! Why won't you speak to me!"

At home, Masako took lessons in flower arranging, calligraphy, and the tea ceremony. She did not understand how anyone could sit on the floor for such long stretches.

"Why do I have to do this?" she exclaimed one day. "I'm not going to be a florist or a sign painter! And I like my tea with milk and sugar!"

"You are going to be a proper Japanese lady," her mother said.

"All I want is to go to college and then have an apartment of my own."

"A young lady needs a husband from a good family."

"A husband! I'd rather have a turtle than a husband!"

"We have hired a very good matchmaker," her mother said.

So they were married in Yokohama and made a home there. I was their first child.

My father called my mother May, but to everyone else she was Masako. At home they spoke English to each other and Japanese to me. Sometimes my mother wore a kimono, but she never got used to sitting on the floor for very long.

All this happened a long time ago, but even today I always drink my tea with milk and sugar.